GAME

First published 2015 by
A & C Black, an imprint of Bloomsbury Publishing Plc
50 Bedford Square, London, WC1B 3DP

www.bloomsbury.com

A CIP catalogue for this book is available from the British Library

ISBN 978–1–4729–0953–4

Typeset by Newgen Knowledge Works (P) Ltd., Chennai, India
Printed and bound in Great Britain by
CPI Group (UK) Ltd, Croydon, CR0 4YY

1 3 5 7 9 10 8 6 4 2

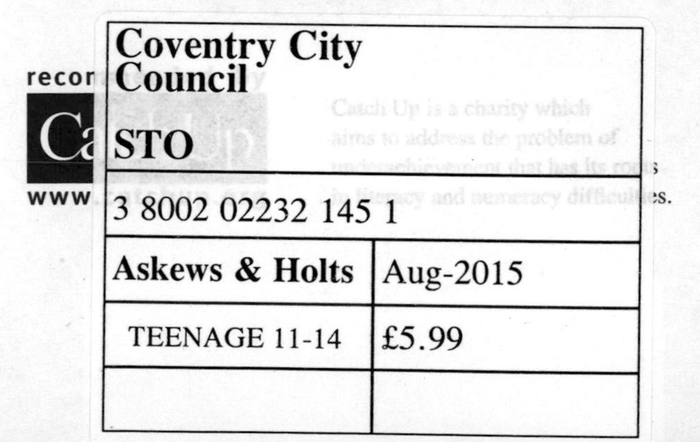

DEADLY GAME

BETH CHAMBERS

ILLUSTRATED BY
SEAN LONGCROFT

A & C BLACK
AN IMPRINT OF BLOOMSBURY
LONDON NEW DELHI NEW YORK SYDNEY

Contents

Chapter One

In my town, being twelve was like being in prison.

I had been twelve for three hundred and sixty-three days, ten hours, fourteen minutes and nine seconds. In two days I'd be thirteen.

I couldn't wait.

From the moment I had reached my twelfth birthday, I was watched all the time. I couldn't even go to the toilet without being watched. Okay, maybe it wasn't *quite* that bad. But trust me, if you were twelve, Redrock was *the* worst place to live in.

It was a miracle I had got out on my own that day. My parents thought I was with my friend, Jack. They didn't know that his parents had taken him to London for his birthday. He was going to be twelve the very next day.

I had told my parents that Jack and his mum were waiting for me at the end of our drive. I felt bad for lying. But I had to get out. I just wanted to be on my own for a bit. I had been watched every minute for almost a year. I knew how a prisoner must feel. It meant you never had your own space. You were never alone

Now, I had to hurry back. The quickest way back home was through the churchyard. I didn't want to go in, but I had no choice.

I walked past rows of crumbling gravestones. At the other end of the graveyard I reached The Wall.

The Wall was made from smooth white stones. It looked out of place in the old graveyard with its old grey church. Half of the stones had writing carved on them. The other half were bare. I wondered whose names would end up on them. Not mine. I was two days away from being twelve. Then I would be safe. Two days until I got my life back.

There was a name carved on each stone. Each name was different. But all the stones said the same thing after the name. *Missing, aged 12.*

No bodies had ever been found. These stones were for the missing Redrock children.

I reached up and traced my fingers over the oldest stone. *In memory of Charlie Hay. Missing, aged 12, June 1974. Not forgotten.*

The curse on the town began in 1974, after Charlie went missing. Children vanished. Only children who were twelve years old. No one knew why. No one knew where or how the children were taken.

And no one ever talked about Charlie Hay. I asked my dad what happened the day Charlie went missing, but Dad wouldn't say anything. Dad and Charlie were best friends, back then. No wonder he didn't like talking about it.

I turned to go. The graveyard scared me. It reminded me that there might be a crazy serial killer in Redrock and I was still twelve years old.

Chapter Two

It was not going to be easy to get back into my home.

I worked my way around to the back of the house, looking for an open door or window. Of course, I could have rung the doorbell.

But then I would have had to explain why Jack and his mum weren't with me. I was not allowed to be on my own. Every Redrock child that had been taken had vanished when they were on their own. That was why no one had ever been able to work out who, or what, took the children

I went around the corner of my house and collided with my mother. She had just put the washing on the line.

She frowned. "What are you doing?"

"I, uh. . . wanted to use the back door for a change," I muttered.

Mum's frown deepened. "How long have you been back? Why are you on your own?"

"Only a few seconds," I said. I didn't answer the second question.

"I'm going to call Jack's mother and ask why she didn't hand you over to me." Mum narrowed her eyes. "It's not like her."

"It was only for a couple of seconds," I repeated. All hell would break loose if my mum called Jack's mum. "And I'm safe, aren't I?" I said. I picked up the laundry basket. If I amazed Mum by how helpful I was being, she might stop asking questions.

I pretended not to notice the look of surprise on her face and I walked into the kitchen. My dad was cooking a stir-fry.

"Hey, Scott. You do know you have a laundry basket in your hand?" he joked.

I pulled a face and dropped the basket on the floor. I went into the lounge where my sister was watching TV. "Where's Jack?" she asked, with a hopeful look on her face.

Sometimes, I thought she liked Jack more than she liked me.

"Not here," I said and I picked up the remote control and changed channels.

"Mum!" Emily shouted.

I threw a cushion at her. She threw it back. Before I could chuck it again, she jumped on me. It was amazing how heavy an eight-year-old girl could be. She balled her hands into fists and started punching my chest.

"You're such a pain, Scott," she yelled. "All you ever do is boss me about."

"Yeah, yeah, whatever," I said, pushing her off. She stared up at me, her hair in a tangle over her face. I knew I should calm her down. Emily got really bad asthma attacks. Getting upset made it much worse.

I knew I should leave her alone. But, as I left the room, I turned and said, "I'm going now so you can cry." Then, I shut the door as she screamed.

I went upstairs to my room and turned on my games console. I lost track of time. When there was a knock on my door, I thought it was Emily, back for round two. I picked up a pillow off my bed and held it above my head to hit her.

But it wasn't Emily standing there. It was my dad. He looked at me. His face was very serious.

"It's Emily," he said. "She's sick."

Chapter Three

Had Emily got sick because I had teased her?

"What's wrong with her?" I asked, trying not to look guilty.

"She's having a bad asthma attack," said Dad. His dark hair fell untidily over his face. "We have to get her to hospital right now. Come on!"

I did not want to go to the hospital. My parents might ask me what I had been doing with Emily.

"I don't want to go," I said. "I'll stay here."

"Not on your own," said Dad.

"Molly will come over from next door," I said." Dad did not look pleased. But he nodded his head. There was no time to argue. "Call her now," he said

Molly came over with a teddy bear. "Emily might like him. I broke my arm when I was nine and he came to hospital with me," she said. "He's my good luck bear."

Chapter Four

I turned my head. Behind me, I could see the dark outline of a man in a hat. I tried to jump off my bed but my legs and arms felt as if they were pinned down. I wanted to cry for help but I couldn't make a sound.

The man leaned over me. His breath was stale. "It's a bit like feeling dead, isn't it?" he whispered. "You can't move, you can't talk. But at least you can breathe. Not like your poor sister."

There was a crushing feeling in my chest. I tried to breathe but couldn't draw in any air. The band of pain grew tighter. I couldn't bear it.

"I'm going to die," I thought.

Suddenly my airways opened and I gasped.

"It's not nice, is it?" the man said. His voice was close to my ear. "But you can fix it for her. You can make Emily's illness go away. Then she will be as healthy as you."

He clicked his fingers and I found I could talk. "How?" I said.

"By playing a game with me," he replied. He spoke in a rasping voice. It sounded amused. "How about it? Just one night. One game, and if you beat me I will give you whatever you want. Of course, you don't have to cure your sister. You can have anything: money, fame, adventure. . ."

I thought about having a huge house with sports cars parked outside. If I were super rich, I could pay for the best doctors in the world to make Emily better.

Then I remembered the crushing pain of not being able to breathe.

If I won, I could

never felt that kind of

I wanted to agree. Bu

a trap. This was what happ

kids in Redrock: this strange

to play a game. I thought of all

twelve-year-olds who must have

this offer and who never came back.

"What happens to me if I lose?" I a

"No one ever dies. I can promise you

replied the man.

"But I won't come home again?" I asked

The stranger shrugged. "Maybe your sister won't come home this time either," he said.

ore I knew what I was doing, the were out of my mouth. “Done,” I said. lay.”

Moonlight poured in through my window. t up the man. He had a pale face with rk, dead eyes. It was a face that looked as it had never smiled. But he’d painted on a bright red grin that stretched from one cheek to the other.

He opened up his oversized jacket and closed it around me. Then, the room began to spin.

Chapter Five

I fell onto something soft and wet. I was in a huge orange dome. There was a wooden table in the middle of the dome. Sitting round the edge of the table were twelve life size dolls. Their eyes stared ahead.

I could have sworn I saw one of them blink.

"Scott?" said a voice. "You too, huh?"

I looked up in shock and saw my friend Jack leaning against a pillar. Next to him were Anna and Tom, twins who were in our class at school.

Tom was a total geek. He was always sucking up to our teacher. He made the rest of us look like slackers. Anna was lazy. She copied everything off Tom in class. She got him to do her homework. She wasn't stupid. She was just smart enough to get someone else to do the work.

Jack reached out his hand to pull me up off the floor.

"I thought you were in London?" I asked.

"He came to me in my hotel room," said Jack. His dark hair was rumpled and he was wearing red pyjamas. "He said if I play he'll give me anything I want. I'm glad you're all here as well. We can help each other, right?"

A laugh cut through the air. It was the man. "I said *if you win* you can have anything you want. But there can be only one winner. There's no such thing as friends in the Prankster's game."

Then the man called the Prankster snapped his fingers. An opening appeared in the dome. We followed him out and stepped into darkness. The only light came from the dome. I glanced back at it. It was an enormous pumpkin.

"A pumpkin? Isn't that a bit corny?" Anna asked, sounding bored. She rolled her eyes and shook back her long blonde hair.

I found myself liking her a bit more. She had guts, talking like that to the Prankster.

He snapped his fingers again. A shower of golden sparks appeared in the dark. They formed a group of glowing words.

Beyond the valley lies
A beacon near the skies.
Here can be claimed the prize,
But only by the wise.
The losers will rue the day
They ever decided to play.
Forever will they regret
The day that they said "yes".

So I had to be the first one to the beacon to win. "That's all we've got to do? Get to the beacon first?" I asked the Prankster. He was watching us. He folded his arms and I noticed that his hands were covered in long red scars.

"Whoever gets to the beacon first wins the game," he said. "Get there before sunrise, or you will all lose. I will be waiting for you." He gave a low mocking bow and walked away into the night.

Tom looked upset. "I don't like the sound of what happens to the losers."

We all went silent. None of us wanted to look at each other.

I could tell that we were all going to do whatever it took to win.

Chapter Six

My eyes had got used to the gloom. Now I could see what was around me. In the distance, I saw a mountain and on the top of it was a column. That had to be the beacon.

I couldn't look at Jack, knowing that this was goodbye. I raced down the slope that led to dense woodland.

Someone shoved me from behind and I crashed onto the ground. It knocked the air out of me.

"Loser," Anna sneered. She leaped over me and raced ahead. Tom was sticking close to her heels.

I rolled over and found Jack looming over me. I wondered if he would shout at me for taking off. Instead he tugged me up on my feet.

"Come on," he said. "Stick with me. I'll protect you from her."

We hurried down the hillside, leaving the giant pumpkin behind. "So," I puffed. "What made you agree to play the game?"

Jack leaped over a ditch. "I've always wanted to be president of the United States. It was too good an offer to turn down."

I stared at him and almost fell into the ditch. "Really?"

"No, you idiot." Jack laughed. "I'm doing it for Emily. If I win I'm going to make sure she gets cured."

Whoa. I knew Jack had always loved Emily, but you have to love someone a lot to do this for them. I tried to forget that for a tiny moment I had been tempted to choose money rather than a cure for Emily.

We reached the tree line and I pointed out a narrow path. "That way," I said.

Before Jack could respond, we heard a noise that gave me goosebumps.

It was a scream.

Anna's scream.

Chapter Seven

We followed the sound, twisting to avoid branches. “Anna!” Jack yelled. “Where are you?”

I understood why he was shouting but it added to my fear. Whatever was making Anna scream now knew where we were, too.

"I'm here," shrieked Anna from up ahead. "Help me."

We rounded a bend and came into a clearing. I could see clearly in the moonlight. I skidded to a halt at what was in front of us.

Anna was kneeling on a wooden platform. Above the platform was a gallows. From the gallows hung a rope with a noose. Tom was hanging from the noose. Above the wooden post circled a flock of ravens. They cawed to each other before swooping at us, their wings brushing against our heads.

I ducked and covered my head with my arms.

"Help us," Anna cried. She struggled to hold Tom up to take the pressure of the rope off his neck.

"What happened?" Jack yelled. He jumped onto the platform to help Anna.

Glowing words were fading in the air: a message from the Prankster. I stood up and ignored the ravens who were madly beating their wings.

I read the words aloud.

You must choose,
Who must lose.
Say it quick,
The clock does tick.

It took me a moment to understand. Tom had chosen the hangman's rope for himself, not one of us. "You saved us?"I asked.

Anna looked down at me. Her eyes flashed with anger. "Of course he didn't," she snapped. "He chose *you*, and the moment he did, the rope went around his neck."

Chapter Eight

I put my hands over my ears. All I could hear was the harsh cries of the birds. I needed to think. This didn't make sense. Not if the Prankster were to be believed. I repeated his promise in my mind. *No one ever dies.*

I had to keep playing the game. Tom might have lost but he would be okay. He had to be. The Prankster had promised. No one would die.

"I'm sorry," I muttered. "I've got to keep going." I didn't dare look at Jack, who was helping to hold Tom up. As I stumbled away I heard Anna say, "I'll win, Tom, I promise, and when I do I'll wish for you to be free."

My heart began to pound. If Anna won, Jack and I would be stuck here forever.

Behind me, I heard a long drawn out scream. I glanced over my shoulder. What I saw made me freeze.

Tom's face was changing. His nose lengthened and sharpened. He reached up to touch his face but before his fingers made contact with his skin they closed together. His fingertips began to sprout quills. He flapped his arms as they grew glistening black feathers. "No!" he shouted. His voice broke and out of his mouth sounded a harsh caw. His body began to shrink until his jumper swallowed him up. Anna and Jack stared helplessly, as Tom's clothes fell into a heap on the ground. A moment later, a raven emerged and hopped over to Anna.

"Tom?" she whispered.

The raven beat its wings and soared into the air. It passed over my head and stared down at me through terrified blue eyes.

Tom's eyes.

"No one dies," I remembered the Prankster saying, but he did not say in what form they would live.

Chapter Nine

Without warning, the ravens suddenly flocked together. They flew off with squawks of alarm.

I looked to see what had scared them and saw a thick black cloud moving in our direction.

It covered Anna and Jack before coming down on me. Wings brushed against my cheeks and sharp claws tangled in my hair. Bats! I glimpsed pointed fangs, and then the ground gave way beneath us.

The bats rose up into the sky as we fell down a steep hill.

The air was knocked out of me as I rolled over and over. At last, I stopped. There was a loud noise of rushing water.

I staggered to my feet and felt blood trickle down my face. It was hard to move but I had to keep going. I had to get to the beacon first.

I walked a few feet and stumbled over something. Looking down, I made out Jack's pale face. "Here." I held out my hand.

Jack stared past me at a new burst of sparks. Anna joined us, brushing the dirt off her clothes. She read out the words as they began to form.

"By stepping stones,
Or weeping tree,
is room for two,
but not for three."

Anna narrowed her eyes. "Later, losers," she said

She shoved us both aside and raced down to the edge of the river. On the opposite bank was a willow tree, which slowly bent until it stretched like a bridge across the water.

Anna splashed into the river. She grasped the tree's branches and scrambled onto its trunk. She clung on as it slowly straightened, taking her to the opposite side.

I turned to Jack but he was no longer there. He was down by the river, balanced on the first of a row of stones. When he stepped onto the second stone the first sank under the water.

He glanced back at me. "I'm sorry. I can't be stuck here, Scott. I just can't do it."

Panic rushed over me. I was going to be trapped in the game, just like all the others.

Chapter Ten

I plunged into the water. It was freezing cold. I fought against the strong current. White froth crashed over my head and I was dragged under the surface. My lungs felt as if they were about to explode. For a moment, I wanted to give in, to stop fighting and accept it was over.

Then the current let me go. I shot up to the surface. The opposite bank was near so I swam as hard as I could. I sobbed with relief when my hands touched the river bank. I dragged myself up onto the bank, and spewed out a mouthful of water.

I knew I should get up to chase after the others but my legs were too weak.

"Scott?" It was Jack's voice. He sounded very scared.

I looked around. Jack was on the final stepping stone. Why didn't he jump off?

Before I could ask, I heard Anna whimper. She was clinging to the tree trunk.

Making a huge effort, I got to my feet. My sodden clothes clung to me.

Jack and Anna stayed where they were. I glanced around. Maybe there was something lurking in the nearby bushes.

"Anna!" Jack yelled.

I turned back to Anna and saw her skin was turning dark. Her arms jerked above her head and twisted into the shape of branches. "Help me," she moaned. "Please. . ." Her cries broke off as her face froze and she could no longer move her lips.

I stumbled over to her but my fingers touched rough bark. It was too late. Her body had taken on the form of the tree. The human shape of her could just be made out in the curves and twists of the wood. A faint breeze stirred through the branches, before whispering past my ear. "Don't. . . leave. . . me."

I bent over and threw up. When I finally stood up, I looked for Jack. He was up to his waist in the water.

"Jump to the bank," I yelled, racing towards him.

The tears running down Jack's cheeks glinted in the moonlight. "I can't move," he whispered.

By the time I reached the bank, he had sunk beneath the water. I dropped to my knees and stared down. Against the river bed I could just make out the faint shape of Jack's body. I plunged my hand into the water but came back with nothing but a handful of silt. Through the murky water I could see what looked like two shining stones. I knew what they were. They were Jack's eyes, staring upward at a sky that was forever out of his reach.

I felt a rush of hate towards the Prankster. I didn't know how, but I was going to make him pay for what he'd done.

Above the mountain the light was beginning to soften. Dawn was about to break.

I had to get to the beacon.

But before I could move I heard a long growl.

I wasn't alone.

Chapter Eleven

For a moment I considered jumping into the river. Then, I thought about what had happened to Jack.

I turned around and saw three huge black dogs.

Their mouths were open, showing long sharp teeth. They strained forward as if waiting for a signal to attack. Their eyes were small and mean and burned bright red.

Hellhounds.

A shower of sparks appeared above the dogs but, instead of forming words, the sparks settled on the ground to show a path for me to follow. The dogs' ears flattened and they inched away from the glowing path. It was clear that they wouldn't go anywhere near it.

I raised my foot to step on to the path. Then, I thought of something. Tom, Anna and Jack all got trapped in the game after deciding to save themselves.

Shaking with fear, I turned to face the dogs again and stepped towards them.

The dogs lunged forward, drool falling from their open mouths.

I squeezed my eyes shut, pointed my finger and yelled, "Get lost. Go home, now!"

I heard a faint whine. A moment later, I opened my eyes and saw the dogs trotting away, their tails tucked between their legs.

I'd done it! I had outwitted the Prankster. Now, all I had to do was get to the beacon before the sun appeared.

I climbed the mountain and tried not to think about the others. Somehow, I had to find a way of getting the Prankster to let them go.

The beacon came into sight. It was just a column of stone. I half ran, half stumbled towards it as the first glimpse of the sun appeared. I fell onto the steps at the base of the column and rested my face against the smooth stone.

I've done it. I've won.

At the foot of the column was a plaque. On it were the words, *In memory of Charlie Hay. Missing. Aged 12.*

A shadow fell over me. I turned and looked into the Prankster's grinning face. "So, you won," he said. "Want to choose your heart's desire?"

My desire right then was to punch him in the nose. What had my friends and all the other missing kids from Redrock done to deserve being trapped in the Prankster's world?

I jerked my head at the beacon. "What does Charlie Hay have to do with you?"

Under the painted grin, the Prankster's lips twisted. "He has everything to do with me," he replied. He put his face close to mine. "He *is* me."

Chapter Twelve

"You're Charlie Hay?" I asked. "How?"

"You mean to say that your father didn't tell you?" replied the Prankster.

"He doesn't know," I said. How had Charlie Hay become the Prankster and made this world? "You vanished. What happened?"

The Prankster stared into the distance. “We all went up onto the moor one day. The others wanted to play dares. They were always playing tricks on me. I was the youngest and the smallest. When we got onto the moor, they dared me to put on a blindfold and walk forward. I fell into a bog and began to sink. That was the trick they wanted to play on me. I pulled off the blindfold and reached for an overhanging tree branch. I managed to pull myself out. I wanted to get back at them. I wanted them to think I’d sunk all the way down into the bog, so I crept away.

I didn't know that there was an old mine shaft nearby. The rotten boards that covered it broke under my weight and I fell through. When I landed I broke my leg. I couldn't climb out. I could hear the others calling for me but they couldn't hear me yelling back. In the end they went away. But instead of getting help, they left me. I believed almost to the end that they would come back. That they'd save me. . ."

I shook my head. My dad would never have left if he'd thought Charlie was still alive. Dad thought Charlie had been sucked into the bog. I wondered whether Dad and his friends had been too afraid to own up about what had happened to Charlie.

"And so," the Prankster said, "over the years I've taken my revenge on all of the twelve-year-olds of Redrock."

"You're sick," I told him. "Really sick."

The Prankster narrowed his eyes. "No," he told me. "I'm just clever. And I'm kind too. I never got a choice, but I'm going to let you have one. What's your heart's desire? What is it that you want?"

I want my friends back.

I want my sister to never get sick again.

I want you to go away forever.

I want to go home. . .

I knew I couldn't choose any of them. I had worked out the twisted rules of the Prankster's game. The moment anyone took the choice offered to them they were trapped by it. The only way to win was not to choose at all. There never was going to be the chance of winning my heart's desire. But at least I had worked it out. At least I would rob the Prankster of another victim and beat him at his own game.

“I’m not going to choose anything,” I said. “And when I go home, I’m going to tell them everything. No one will ever be tricked into playing your game again.”

There was a long pause while the Prankster thought about my words. “Well now,” he finally replied, taking off his hat and placing it on my head. “Aren’t you the spoil-sport? Like father like son.” His eyes had an evil glint. “So,” he said in a sing-song voice.

“*The game is done,*
but who has won?
One thing’s true,
it isn’t you.
You made a choice.”

“No I didn’t,” I protested.

The Prankster tipped back his head and laughed. "You chose not to choose. Let's see how you feel after you've spent time in my shoes." He began to fade and as I reached out to grab him, my fingers connected with nothing but air.

I reached up to take off the hat but, as I did, I saw something red. I had large red clown shoes on my feet. I stumbled down the mountain, back to the river. I dropped to my knees and stared down at my image in the water.

It was then I realised I had lost everything. The Prankster had made sure I was trapped after all.

The last trick had been played on me.

It wasn't my reflection I was staring at.

It was a clown's.